# The Boxcar Children Mysteries

# THE CREATURE IN OGOPOGO LAKE

### created by
## GERTRUDE CHANDLER WARNER

*Illustrated by Robert Papp*

ALBERT WHITMAN & Company
Morton Grove, Illinois

The Creature in Ogopogo Lake
created by Gertrude Chandler Warner;
illustrated by Robert Papp.

ISBN 13: 978-0-8075-1336-1 (hardcover)
ISBN 10: 0-8075-1336-9 (hardcover)
ISBN 13: 978-0-8075-1337-8 (paperback)
ISBN 10: 0-8075-1337-7 (paperback)

*Cover art by Robert Papp.*

For more information about Albert Whitman & Company,
visit our web site at www.albertwhitman.com.

# Contents

# THE CREATURE IN
# OGOPOGO LAKE

# CHAPTER 1

# A Monster Lurks

"Do you think it's true?" asked six-year-old Benny. The youngest Alden had his nose pressed up against the window of their rental car. "Is there really a monster in Ogopogo Lake?" His eyes were huge.

"You mean, Okanagan Lake," corrected twelve-year-old Jessie, who often acted like a mother to her younger brother and sister. "Ogopogo is the name of the famous Canadian monster that lives in Okanagan Lake."

"I like *Ogopogo* Lake better," insisted Benny. "After all, it's the monster's home."

Henry, who was sitting up front beside Grandfather, smiled back at his little brother. "There's no real proof the monster exists, Benny." Henry was fourteen. He was the oldest of the Aldens.

Grandfather slowed down for a curve in the road. "They've even used underwater cameras to search for the creature," he said, "but nothing's turned up. Of course, that doesn't stop folks from keeping their eyes peeled. Everybody hopes to catch a glimpse of Ogopogo."

"Good thing I brought along my binoculars." Benny grinned.

"And I packed my camera," put in Violet, who was ten. Photography was one of Violet's hobbies. She almost always brought her camera along when they went on vacations.

James Alden and his four grandchildren—Henry, Jessie, Violet, and Benny—had just arrived for a holiday in the Okanagan Valley in British Columbia. They were on their way to the Ogopogo Resort in Peachland. Grandfather was renting a cabin from his good friend Abby Harmon.

"Should I check the map, Grandfather?" asked Jessie, who was the best map-reader in the family.

"That's okay, Jessie. I haven't forgotten how to get to Peachland."

"Oh, that's right," said Jessie. "You used to come here all the time. Didn't you, Grandfather?"

"We came every summer when I was growing up. My parents always rented a cabin from the Harmon family. Abby was about my age, and we soon became great friends."

"And you never lost touch," said Violet. "Right, Grandfather?"

"No, we didn't." Grandfather smiled at his youngest granddaughter through the rear view mirror. "We've been pen pals ever since. After Abby's father died," he went on, "she inherited the Ogopogo Resort. She still rents out cabins and runs a small gift shop."

"Sounds like fun," said Henry.

"Abby *does* enjoy it," said Grandfather. "But..."

"But what?" asked Violet.

"The place is getting old," Grandfather answered. "From what I hear, it's badly in need of repair. I'm afraid, with all the new resorts springing up everywhere, people aren't coming to stay at Abby's cabins."

Henry looked puzzled. "Why doesn't she just spruce the place up a bit?"

"Abby doesn't have the money for repairs, Henry. In fact, she's even been thinking of selling the resort."

"How sad!" Violet sighed.

"Abby hasn't made her mind up yet, Violet," Grandfather told her. "But someone said he would buy it. She's trying to decide what to do."

"That must be hard for Abby," Jessie said. "To make a decision like that, I mean."

Grandfather nodded. "The Ogopogo Resort is the only home she's ever known."

"We kept *our* old home," Benny said. "Thanks to you, Grandfather."

After their parents died, the four Alden children had run away. When they discovered an abandoned boxcar in the woods, they made it their home. Then their grandfather found them and brought them to live with him in his big white house in Greenfield. He even surprised his grandchildren by giving the boxcar a special place in the backyard. The Aldens often used the boxcar as a clubhouse.

They were all enjoying the car ride as they looked out the windows and saw the beautiful green orchards and vineyards. In the distance, dry brown hills were scattered with tall trees. Benny was the first to break the silence.

"I was just wondering," he said, sounding a bit uneasy. "What exactly does it look like?"

Grandfather seemed puzzled, but only for a moment. "Oh, you mean Ogopogo.

Well, it's supposed to be a long, snake-like creature with a head like a sheep. Some people say it's a plesiosaur."

Benny made a face. "A *what?*"

"A plesiosaur," said Grandfather. "A creature left over from the dinosaur era, Benny. It was thought to be extinct for more than one million years."

"Has Abby ever seen the leftover dinosaur?" Violet asked.

"Not that I know of," answered Grandfather. Then he chuckled. "Back when we were kids, we thought we'd spotted Ogopogo swimming in the lake. Turned out to be logs floating in the water."

"Ogopogo is a funny name for a monster," Jessie noted.

Henry nodded. "Not exactly a scary name, that's for sure."

"Ogopogo is supposed to be quite harmless," Grandfather informed them. "If there *is* a monster in the lake, it seems to keep pretty much to itself."

Benny looked relieved to hear this.

"I bet Ogopogo doesn't like being around strangers," guessed Violet. She was shy, and meeting new people often made her nervous.

As Grandfather slowed to a stop beside a fruit and vegetable market, Benny clapped his hands. "You read my mind, Grandfather!" he chirped. "I was just getting hungry."

"Benny, you're *always* hungry!" Henry teased. The youngest Alden was known for his appetite. They all got out and stretched their legs.

"I thought we'd stock up for the week," said Grandfather as they went inside. "The Okanagan Valley is famous for its fruit."

In no time at all, they were all busy filling their baskets. Jessie was checking out the cherries when she heard someone talking on a cell phone nearby.

"Of course, I'll do whatever it takes!" a woman was saying, sounding annoyed. "Look, I need this sale. I won't come in second. Not again. Not this year!"

Jessie didn't mean to eavesdrop. But from

where she was standing, it was impossible not to overhear.

"I know how to handle Abby." The woman was talking loudly now. "I'll get that rundown resort sold, if it's the last thing I do!" With that, the woman pocketed her cell phone and hurried away.

Violet couldn't help wondering if she'd heard right. Was that smartly dressed woman with the dangly earrings talking about *Abby Harmon?*

CHAPTER 2

# Hidden Treasure

After making another stop for groceries, the Aldens were soon heading into Peachland. Everywhere they looked, tourists were strolling along the sidewalks and in and out of the shops and restaurants beside the sparkling blue lake.

"The resort's just up ahead," Grandfather told the children. "Keep your eyes peeled, everybody. If I remember right, there should be a sign hanging from a tree out front."

It wasn't long before sharp-eyed Benny

cried out, "There it is!" He pointed to a huge pine tree where three signs were hanging, hooked together, one on top of the other—OGOPOGO RESORT, CABINS FOR RENT, and OGOPOGO GIFT SHOP.

"Way to go, Benny!" said Jessie, as they turned into the gravel driveway. "Those signs aren't easy to spot from the road. The paint's all faded and peeling."

At the end of the driveway, Grandfather parked the car beside the long grass. Everyone piled out. Benny looked over at the line of cabins nestled among the pines.

"One, two, three, four, five, six," he counted. "Which cabin does Abby live in?"

"Abby lives over there." Grandfather nodded in the direction of a small building where a mustard-colored bench stood beneath a large plate-glass window. The sign above the door read: OGOPOGO GIFT SHOP.

Benny raised his eyebrows. "Abby lives in a *store?*"

"She has a small place in the back of the shop, Benny," Grandfather explained, as he led the way across a lawn covered with dandelions. "Let's go say hello."

As they stepped inside, a bell jingled above the door. A woman looked over as she tucked her short silver hair behind her ear. Her face broke into a smile as soon as she saw her old friend.

"James!" She rushed out from behind the counter. "It's been so long!"

"Much *too* long," said Grandfather, returning his friend's warm hug. "Abby, I want you to meet my grandchildren— Henry, Jessie, Violet, and Benny."

They all shook hands. "It's very nice to meet you," Jessie said politely, speaking for them all.

Benny glanced around. "You sure have lots of Ogopogo stuff in here."

Violet followed Benny's gaze. Everywhere she looked, she could see the famous monster on everything from posters to T-shirts.

Abby laughed. "That's our claim to fame

around here, Benny. Peachland is known as Ogopogo's home."

The four Alden children looked at each other in surprise. "Ogopogo lives in the town?" Benny asked in disbelief. "I thought he lived in the lake."

"Actually, he lives in an underwater cave just across the lake from town," Abby replied. "At least, that's what they say." She pulled a set of keys from her pocket. "I was just about to close up shop. Why don't I walk you over to your cabin?"

"Sure thing." Grandfather gave her a cheery smile.

"By the way," Abby said, "how does a picnic supper by the lake sound? I'm planning a get-together tonight."

Grandfather thought it sounded great. So did everyone else.

"I chose the cabin at the far end for you," said Abby. They followed a stone path that looped its way around the gift shop. "I've been airing it out, but...I'm afraid it still smells a bit musty in there."

Grandfather waved that away. "I'm sure it'll be just fine, Abby."

Benny, who had raced ahead, suddenly called out from the cabin porch. "Come and see this!" He sounded excited.

"What is it, Benny?" asked Henry, taking the steps two at a time.

The youngest Alden pointed to a large wooden carving of a green, snakelike creature with a head like a sheep.

"Wow!" Henry nodded approvingly. "That's pretty cool."

"There's an Ogopogo carving on every porch," said Abby, coming up behind them. "Patch O'Brien was quite an artist."

"Patch?" Benny said. "That's a funny name."

"His real name was Patrick O'Brien," Abby explained. "But Patch always suited him better." She paused for a moment. There was a faraway look in her eye. "I don't think I ever saw my old friend in anything but patched-up clothes."

"Oh, I get it." Benny nodded. "Patch was

his nickname because he wore patches."

"Yes—exactly," said Abby. "It's been a few years since he passed away," she added. "But I still miss him."

Violet didn't like to hear the note of sadness in Abby's voice. She was trying to think of something cheery to say when Jessie spoke up.

"It looks like Patch was an expert carver," she said.

"Oh, yes!" Abby's face brightened. "And you know, he made an especially wonderful carving of Ogopogo just for me. He left it to me in his will," she said, "along with his old boat, and—" She stopped herself in mid-sentence.

"And what, Abby?" Benny wanted to know.

Abby hesitated, then laughed a little. "Well, this is going to sound strange," she said, "but Patch also left me something rather odd."

The four Alden children were instantly curious. "What was it?"

"A riddle," said Abby. "It's supposed to lead to a treasure."

Henry blinked in surprise. "A *treasure?*"

"Wow!" Benny clapped his hands. "If you found a treasure, you could keep the resort!"

Abby smiled. "That's a nice thought, Benny," she said. "The problem is, Patch never owned anything of real value. Of course, I'd love to figure out the riddle," she quickly added. "But...I'm afraid I can't."

"Maybe we can help," Violet offered, and the others nodded.

"You never know," insisted Benny. "The treasure *might* be worth lots and lots of money!"

"My grandchildren are first-class detectives, Abby." Grandfather sounded proud.

"You're welcome to take a shot at it," Abby said, looking pleased. "I'll show you the riddle right after dinner if you like."

At that moment, a maroon car pulled into the driveway. A woman with reddish-brown hair, wearing a business suit, stepped out of the car. Jessie recognized her immediately. It was the woman she'd overheard on the phone at the fruit and vegetable market.

"Oh, that's Rilla Washburn." Abby waved her hand. "Rilla's a local real estate agent. And a good friend," she added.

"I thought you might enjoy these," said Rilla, rushing over with a basket of cherries.

After thanking her friend, Abby quickly introduced everyone.

Rilla gave the Aldens a brisk nod, then turned her attention back to Abby. "So...have you made a decision yet?" she asked in a businesslike voice. "About selling the resort, I mean."

Abby shook her head. "No, I'm afraid I haven't decided yet."

"You haven't decided?" Rilla did not look happy to hear this. "Listen, Abby," she said. "I don't mean to be pushy, but my client made you a very generous offer. If you keep dragging your feet like this, he might back out."

"I know." Abby sighed. "But this whole thing upsets me very much."

Grandfather turned to Rilla. "The resort's been in Abby's family for years," he pointed out. "It's not an easy decision to make."

Rilla frowned. "Well, isn't it lucky Abby has such good friends to look out for her," she said, but it sounded like she didn't think it was lucky at all.

Henry and Jessie looked at each other. Why was Rilla Washburn so unfriendly to them?

"It kills me the way you try to keep this place going, Abby," Rilla continued. "Don't you think it's time to move on?"

"Perhaps," Abby admitted. "But as James said, it's not an easy decision to make. I'm afraid your client will just have to wait."

Rilla looked as if she wanted to argue, but Benny spoke first.

"Don't worry, Abby," he said. "We'll find the treasure, then you can keep the resort."

"What?" Rilla turned around to face the youngest Alden.

"We're going to find a treasure!" Benny was all smiles. "The one Patch left for Abby."

Rilla threw her head back and laughed. "You must be kidding! Patch O'Brien never had a nickel to his name. Everybody knows that."

"But—" Benny began.

"No buts about it!" snapped Rilla. "Oh, I've heard those stories before—how Patch wasn't as poor as he let on. But you know what? That's about as crazy as believing in a lake monster. Absolute rubbish! That's all it is!" She turned to Abby. "Trust me, Abby. The sooner you decide to sell, the better."

"That's a very determined lady," Grandfather said, as Rilla walked away.

Abby unlocked the cabin door. "Yes, that's probably why she's such a good salesperson. You know, she's been runner-up for the top sales award seven years in a row. I'm keeping my fingers crossed she'll win this year. The award ceremony's just a few weeks away."

Inside, the Aldens found an old couch and some worn-out chairs grouped together around a crumbling stone fireplace. Tattered yellow curtains hung from the windows, and faded green wallpaper covered the walls.

Grandfather looked around. "Things haven't changed a bit."

Abby laughed. "That's just the problem, James."

"Well, I like it here!" said Benny.

Abby smiled warmly at the youngest Alden. "I wish everybody felt that way, Benny," she said. "I'd better go and let you get settled in. Now, don't forget about that picnic supper by the lake," she added, then hurried away.

The four Alden children began to unpack groceries while Grandfather napped on the couch.

"I really like Abby," said Violet.

"So do I." Jessie nodded, as she opened the refrigerator and put the lettuce away. "I sure hope we can find that treasure for her."

Benny passed a box of cornflakes to Henry. "Rilla Washburn doesn't think there *is* a treasure," he said with a frown.

"Well, it does seem odd," Henry had to admit. He put the cereal into the cupboard.

"How could Patch O'Brien have left Abby a treasure in his will if he was flat broke?"

"That's a good question, Henry," said Jessie. "Still, it's worth checking out."

"I hope Abby doesn't sell the resort before we have time to find the treasure," Benny said.

"Rilla sure was trying to get Abby to sell as soon as possible," said Violet. "I wonder why?"

"She's a real estate agent," Henry pointed out. "Whenever one of her clients buys or sells property, she makes money. That's how she earns her living."

"That's true, Henry," said Violet. "But she's also Abby's friend. Don't you think she should back off and give Abby a chance to make up her mind?"

"She won't back off until Abby sells the resort," said Jessie.

"What makes you so sure?" Violet asked in surprise.

Jessie quickly told them about the phone conversation she'd overheard at the fruit and vegetable market. "Rilla said she needs this sale, and that she doesn't want to come in second this year."

Henry nodded. "I bet she was talking about the top sales award."

"I have a hunch," Jessie said after a moment's thought, "that if Abby doesn't sell the resort, Rilla won't win."

"I think you're right," said Violet. "And she plans to do whatever it takes."

"Well, guess what?" said Benny. "We'll do whatever it takes, too—to find the treasure."

"For sure, Benny," said Henry.

CHAPTER 3

# A Sighting

"See that boat over there?" Benny was standing by the water's edge. "The one at the end of the dock?"

The four Alden children were helping Abby get ready for the picnic. Henry looked over. "What about it, Benny?"

"I bet that's the one Abby was talking about," guessed Benny. "The one Patch left to her, I mean."

"You're right on the mark, Benny," Abby said, coming up behind them. She was carrying a bowl filled with pasta salad. "That's the *Seven Seas.*"

"What a great name for a boat!" said Jessie. She made room for Abby's salad among the plastic containers and covered dishes.

Abby nodded. "Patch spent most of his life sailing the seven seas searching for treasures. When he finally saved up enough to buy that old boat, he decided the *Seven Seas* was the perfect name for her."

"Was Patch a *pirate?*" Benny's eyes were wide.

"No, nothing like that, Benny." Abby couldn't help smiling. "When ships sailed the oceans long ago," she explained, "they were often caught in terrible storms. Sometimes the ships would sink to the bottom of the ocean. Patch was part of a diving crew that searched for lost treasures on sunken ships."

"How exciting!" said Violet.

"Wow," added Henry.

"Maybe that's what he left you, Abby,"

Benny exclaimed. "One of the treasures he found at sea!"

"That's not likely, Benny," Abby told him. "Patch had nothing but the clothes on his back when he arrived on my doorstep. I'm afraid he never got rich looking for treasures on the ocean floor."

Violet shook her head sadly. "That's a shame."

"Oh, not really, Violet," said Abby. "You see, Patch never placed any importance on money. He always said it was the search he enjoyed."

The Aldens understood. They were never happier than when they were on the trail of clues.

"Did Patch live around here?" Henry wondered.

"Yes, he made his home in one of the cabins," Abby told Henry. "He'd give me a hand with the chores in exchange for a roof over his head. Of course," she added, "I got the better end of that deal."

"Why do you say that, Abby?" asked Violet.

"Because Patch worked very hard. When he wasn't helping me, he was busy painting or carving. And let me tell you, everything he made sold like hotcakes. That's how he bought that old boat."

Just then, Grandfather came down the path, carrying a pitcher of lemonade. "Where do you want this, Abby?"

Abby laughed. "Wherever you can find room, James."

"Who else is coming, Abby?" Jessie asked. She had noticed the two extra places at the table.

"I invited Max Lowe and his son, Adam, to join us," said Abby. "They're staying in the second cabin down from yours."

"Will they be coming soon?" Benny asked hopefully.

"Don't worry, Benny." Jessie smiled at her little brother. "I'm sure we'll be eating before long."

Abby handed the youngest Alden a celery stick with cheese in it. "Here you go, Benny. This should tide you over."

"Hey, save some for us!" a voice called from the lakeside path.

Everyone turned to see a tall man with a tumble of sandy curls walking towards them. Beside him was a boy about Henry's age, his nose peeling from the sun.

"There's enough here to feed an army, Max," Abby said with a grin. Then she introduced the Aldens to Max Lowe and his son, Adam. "We've been talking about the *Seven Seas*," she told them, as everyone crowded around the long picnic table.

"Patch did a great job restoring that old boat," said Max, lifting some food onto his plate. "We sure make good use of it."

Abby nodded. "Max and Adam take folks out Ogopogo hunting," she explained. "Visitors get a tour of the lake and a chance to catch a glimpse of the famous monster."

"Sounds like fun," said Henry. Then he turned to Adam. "I bet you get all kinds of questions about the monster."

Adam nodded. "Everybody wants to know what Ogopogo looks like."

"We tell them as much as we can," added Max.

"They handle the boat tours for me," put in Abby. "In return, they get a free cabin for the summer."

"Adam and I really look forward to getting away from the city in the summer," Max explained.

Grandfather helped himself to the coleslaw. "Sounds like it works out for everyone."

"It sure does," said Adam.

Benny was wondering about something. "Adam, have you ever seen the monster?"

"Nope." Adam smiled at the Aldens. "We've been around the lake about a million times and we haven't spotted anything strange. I don't think there is a monster out there, Benny."

Max put down his fork and looked around at the Aldens. "Why don't we check it out? Who's up for some Ogopogo hunting?"

Henry, Jessie, Violet, and Benny waved their hands high in the air.

Max looked pleased. "How about meeting us at the end of the dock around ten tomorrow morning?"

"Sure," said Jessie. "If that's okay with you, Grandfather."

Grandfather nodded. "You can't pass up a chance like that."

"I'll bring my binoculars," said Benny. He sounded excited.

"And I won't forget about my camera," added Violet.

"Then it's settled." Max looked pleased. "It'll give us a good excuse to take the boat out. It's been a while since we've booked a tour."

"Yes, business has been pretty slow." Abby sighed. "What we need is a good Ogopogo sighting."

Grandfather chuckled. "I imagine that *would* bring the tourists into town."

"Oh, yes," said Abby. "Business always picks up after a report of a strange creature in the water."

"If I remember right," said Grandfather,

"Peachland holds the record for the most sightings. Doesn't it?"

"It sure does." Max reached for the pepper. "Every summer someone around here says they've seen Ogopogo."

"I bet I know why," piped up Benny. "I bet it's because Ogopogo makes his home right across the lake."

"You catch on fast, Benny." Abby smiled at the youngest Alden. "Would you pass the butter, Adam?"

Adam didn't answer. He was staring out at the lake.

"Adam?"

Adam still made no reply. When Abby reached out and put a hand gently on his arm, he suddenly jerked his head around. "Oh!" He seemed to have forgotten where he was.

"You're a million miles away, Adam," said Abby. "What are you thinking about?"

"I'm...um, not feeling very well," Adam said quickly. "Guess I got a bit too much sun today. Is it okay if I go back to the cabin?"

Adam looked over at his father expectantly.

"Go ahead," Max answered, a note of concern in his voice. "I won't be long."

Jessie couldn't help noticing that Adam had eaten every bit of food on his plate. Was he really not feeling well?

"I hope Adam's better by tomorrow," Benny said, as Adam hurried away. "For the Ogopogo hunt, I mean."

"I'm sure he'll be fine," said Max. "The truth is, Adam hasn't been himself lately. I'm afraid he's upset about the resort being sold."

Abby nodded her head sadly. "Believe me, the last thing I want to do is sell my home."

"What if you did some advertising, Abby?" Grandfather suggested. "It might bring in more business."

Henry, Jessie, Violet, and Benny all paid attention when their grandfather spoke. James Alden knew all there was to know about business.

"Yes," agreed Abby. "Advertising would help, James. But it takes money to advertise. And the truth is, I'm pinching pennies right now. Besides," she added, "it's awfully hard to compete with the fancier resorts. Some of them even have waterslides." She let out a long sigh. "Waterslides are very popular right now."

Violet spoke up. "What if we painted the signs out front for you, Abby?" she offered. "Bright colors would really make them stand out."

Grandfather nodded approvingly. "It would certainly catch a tourist's eye."

"That would be wonderful." Abby looked surprised—and pleased. "Are you sure you wouldn't mind?"

"It's fun to paint!" Benny piped up. And Henry and Jessie nodded.

"That's very kind of you," said Abby. "Now, there's a paint store in town, but it's closed tomorrow. Why don't you stop by the gift shop on Monday. I'll give you some money from the cash register, and you can get what you need. Oh!" Abby touched a hand to her mouth. "I almost forgot! I have something for you, Benny."

"For me?" Benny pointed to himself.

Abby reached into her straw bag and pulled out a stuffed Ogopogo. She held it out to the youngest Alden.

Benny was grinning from ear to ear. "Thank you very much!"

"Ogopogo will be good company for Stockings," Violet said, smiling over at her little brother. Stockings was a rag bear made from old socks. Violet and Jessie had made the rag bear for Benny when they were living in the boxcar.

Over dessert, Henry, Jessie, Violet, and Benny took turns telling Abby and Max all about their boxcar days. When they were finished, they gave Abby a hand clearing the picnic table.

After the dishes were finished, Abby led the way into her living room.

"Is that the carving Patch made for you, Abby?" Henry asked. He pointed to the Ogopogo carving beside the fireplace. The carving was attached to a wooden stand.

Abby nodded. "Yes, isn't it wonderful?"

she said with a smile. "Oh, speaking of Patch, why don't I show you that riddle?"

As they made themselves comfortable on the sofa, Abby reached for the photo album on the coffee table. She began flipping through the pages. "Here it is!" She handed a snapshot to Violet.

"Somebody sure likes cats," Violet said, as she studied the photograph of seven cats curled up along a weathered green bench.

"Patch had a real soft spot for them," said Abby. "He was always taking in strays."

"What happened to them?" Benny wanted to know. "After Patch died, I mean."

"Well, I couldn't take them in myself," Abby told him. "You see, they always made me sneeze up a storm. But I made sure they all went to good homes."

Violet passed the photograph to Henry. Henry passed it to Benny. Benny passed it to Jessie. They were each wondering the same thing. What did a snapshot have to do with the riddle?

"Flip it over, Jessie," Abby instructed.

On the back of the photograph, Jessie found a verse printed in black ink.

"What does that say?" Benny asked, checking it out over her shoulder. He was just learning to read.

Jessie read the riddle aloud:

> *An awesome treasure*
> *you can find*
> *with the clue*
> *I've left behind.*

"Wow," said Benny. "That's not much to go on."

"You got that right!" agreed Henry. "What clue did he leave behind?"

"I don't know! I haven't had any luck figuring it out," Abby told them.

"None at all?" asked Violet.

"Zero."

The Aldens looked at one another. How in the world were they going to find the answer to such a strange riddle?

# CHAPTER 4

# *Ogopogo Hunting*

It was dark by the time the Aldens headed back to their cabin. They were just climbing the porch steps when Benny stopped so suddenly that Violet almost bumped into him.

"I forgot Ogopogo!" he cried. "The one Abby gave me."

"Oh, you probably left it by the picnic table," guessed Jessie. "First thing in the morning, we'll—" But Benny was gone before she could finish.

Running full speed along the path, Benny made his way to the water's edge. Sure enough, his stuffed Ogopogo was right where he'd left it—on the bench beside the picnic table. He was just about to hurry back to his brother and sisters when he heard something—a splashing sound. For a long moment, he stood frozen to the spot, his heart pounding. Then, turning slowly, he looked out at the moonlit lake.

"Uh-oh!" The youngest Alden could hardly believe his eyes! In the water, not far from the dock, was the inky outline of a strange creature with three humps, a long neck, and a head like a sheep!

In a flash, Benny wheeled around and raced back along the path. He soon ran smack into Henry, Jessie, and Violet, who were on their way to find him.

Jessie could tell by her little brother's face that something had happened. "What's going on, Benny?" she asked in alarm. "Are you okay?"

Benny pointed to the lake. "Ogopogo!" he

gasped, trying to catch his breath.

Henry wasn't having any of that. "There's no monster out there, Benny," he said firmly.

Violet glanced over at Henry. She knew her older brother was probably right. But Benny's words still sent a chill through her.

"There's only one thing to do," Jessie said, putting a comforting arm around her little brother. "Let's go check it out."

Benny wasn't too sure about this. Still, he followed his brother and sisters back to the picnic table.

"Where did you see it, Benny?" Henry asked him.

"Over there." Benny pointed. "Close to the dock."

But when Henry, Jessie, and Violet looked out at the moonlit lake, they could see nothing but the old boat at the end of the dock. There was no sign of any monster.

"Whatever you saw, Benny," said Henry, "it's gone now."

"It was Ogopogo," Benny insisted, as they

headed back along the path. "I saw it with my own eyes."

"Remember what Grandfather told us, Benny?" Jessie reminded him. "When he was growing up, he was sure he'd spotted Ogopogo, too."

Henry nodded. "But it was just logs floating in the water."

"I'm sure that's all it was, Benny," said Violet. She wasn't really sure, but wanted her little brother to believe she was.

* * * *

The next morning at breakfast, the children decided not to say anything about Ogopogo, but they told their grandfather about the strange riddle. Jessie finished by saying, "Patch left a clue behind, but we don't know where."

Grandfather helped himself to a few strips of crispy bacon. Then he passed the platter to Benny. "It won't be long before you figure things out," he said with a chuckle.

Violet, who was spreading honey on her toast, looked up. "I hope you're right,

Grandfather. We have to find the treasure before Abby sells the resort."

Henry agreed. "We'll get started on it the minute we get back from the boat tour."

"Don't forget to wear your hats," Grandfather reminded them. "The sun can get pretty hot on Okanagan Lake."

"You mean, Ogopogo Lake!" Benny corrected.

Grandfather nodded and smiled.

"Don't worry, Grandfather," Jessie assured him. "We'll be careful."

After leaving the kitchen spic and span, the four Alden children said good-bye to their grandfather, then raced down to the dock. True to their word, Max and Adam were waiting for them by the boat.

"Glad you remembered your camera, Violet," Max told her. "It's a beautiful day for taking pictures."

As Max untied the boat from the rings on the dock, everyone put on their life jackets. Henry and Violet perched on the padded bench seat along one side of the boat. Jessie and Benny sat down across from them.

Max hopped aboard. "Ready to head out?"

Henry gave him the thumbs-up. "We're ready!"

Max started up the motor, sending the seagulls scattering. The *Seven Seas* was soon speeding across the water. For a while, no one said a word. They were all too busy enjoying the warm sun on their faces and the wind in their hair. Every now and again, passing boaters waved as they went by. The Aldens were quick to wave back.

When Jessie looked up, she noticed an airplane trailing a banner behind it. The banner read: FUN IN THE SUN AT THE OGOPOGO RESORT. With that kind of advertising, Jessie realized, it was no wonder Abby's resort was overlooked.

"That's Rattlesnake Island over there," Max told them. "According to local legend, Ogopogo makes its home in an underwater cave somewhere between Rattlesnake Island and Squally Point. Native tribes once called the creature *N'ha-a-itk*, or 'lake demon.'"

Jessie spoke up. "How did it get the name Ogopogo?"

"Somebody wrote a song about the creature years ago," Max explained, "calling it Ogopogo. I guess the name just caught on."

"Grandfather thought he saw Ogopogo once," Benny said, peering through his binoculars. "But it was just logs."

"Just about anything can play tricks on the eye," Max told them. "Even waves from a passing boat or a school of fish. And, of course, there's always the occasional hoax."

Benny frowned. "Hoax?"

Henry explained, "A hoax is when somebody tries to fool people."

"That's right," said Max. "I'm afraid fake Ogopogos crop up every now and again."

Benny said, "It's not nice to trick people."

"No, it isn't," agreed Violet.

Adam, who was sitting up front beside his father, said, "Still, it's possible Nessie's cousin *might* be living in the lake."

"Nessie's cousin?" Benny frowned again.

"That's the name of Scotland's famous

monster," Max explained. "Nessie's supposed to live in a lake called Loch Ness."

"Wow," said Benny. "You mean there's more than one leftover dinosaur?"

Adam shrugged. "Anything's possible."

Jessie looked at him in surprise. At dinner the night before, Adam had made it clear he didn't believe in the monster. Had he changed his mind?

"There's no proof that Nessie exists, Benny," said Henry. "And there's no proof that Ogopogo exists, either."

As Max turned the boat around, Adam looked back at Henry. "If Ogopogo doesn't exist, then why would the government give Ogopogo wildlife status?"

"Wildlife status?" Henry echoed in surprise.

Max nodded. "Ogopogo was given protected wildlife status in 1989. It's illegal to capture or harm it in any way."

Violet looked relieved. "I'm glad."

They were all lost in thought as they made their way back to the dock.

"Thank you so much for the tour," Jessie said, as they scrambled out of the boat. Henry, Violet, and Benny echoed her words.

"You're welcome aboard the *Seven Seas* anytime," Max told them. "I wish we could have stayed out longer, but I'm afraid Adam and I have some errands to run."

"No problem," said Henry, waving good-bye.

As they headed back up the path, Violet said, "How about a swim before lunch?" The others were quick to agree.

After splashing around in the lake for almost an hour, the Aldens went back to the cabin to make lunch.

"I have an idea," said Jessie. "Why don't we eat by the water?" She got out the cold cuts, bread, lettuce, and mustard.

"Sure!" said Benny, washing a handful of cherries under the tap. "I love picnics."

"Maybe we should invite Adam to join us," Violet suggested.

Benny shook his head. "Adam and Max are running errands. Remember?"

"Oh—right," said Violet.

"Speaking of Adam," said Jessie, "the way he was talking today, it sounded as if he believed the monster just might exist. But last night he said he didn't believe in it at all."

"Yeah, that was kind of weird, wasn't it?" said Henry.

"Maybe Adam saw Ogopogo, too." Benny's eyes were wide. "Last night, I mean."

"Maybe," said Jessie. "But I doubt it."

"I think we should concentrate on one mystery at a time," Violet suggested. "Let's work on finding that treasure before it's too late."

Nobody argued. They knew it would take all their detective skills to solve Patch O'Brien's riddle.

CHAPTER 5

## Strike One

"Read it again, Jessie, okay?" said Benny.

Jessie pulled the photograph of Patch O'Brien's cats from her backpack. She read the riddle on the back aloud. *An awesome treasure, / you can find, / with the clue, / I've left behind.* The four Alden children were sitting cross-legged on a small raft tied to the dock.

Benny was puzzled. "How can we find the treasure," he said, "if we don't even know how to find the first clue?"

"It must be somewhere on the property," Violet said thoughtfully.

"But where?" Jessie passed around the napkins. "It'll take forever to search every inch of the resort."

"It isn't much to go on," said Benny. "Just a clue left behind...somewhere." He swallowed the last bite of his sandwich, then washed it down with lemonade.

Jessie looked at Benny in surprise. A funny look came over her face.

"Is anything wrong, Jessie?" asked Violet.

Jessie didn't answer. As she stared down at the riddle, an idea began to form in her mind. Then her face suddenly broke into a smile. "That's it!" she said, more to herself than anyone else.

"Jessie?" said Henry. "What's up?"

"The clue's right here!" Jessie told them, waving the photograph in the air. She sounded excited.

The others stared at Jessie. They looked totally confused.

"Patch left the clue *behind*," said Jessie,

hoping they would catch on. Seeing their puzzled faces, she added, "What's behind the riddle?"

Henry looked even more confused. "I'm not following you, Jessie."

"Wait a minute," said Violet. "Are you talking about the photograph of Patch O'Brien's cats?"

Nodding, Jessie flipped the riddle over. "I have a hunch the clue's hidden somewhere in this photograph."

"But...where?" asked Benny.

"I haven't the slightest idea," Jessie admitted. "But if we put our heads together, maybe we can figure it out."

They took turns studying the photograph—first Jessie, then Benny, then Violet, and finally Henry. On the second time around, Henry said, "That bench looks familiar."

"Really?" Jessie took a closer look. "I don't remember seeing a green bench around anywhere."

"Maybe it isn't green anymore. Take a

look at that crack along the back," said Violet, who had an artist's eye for detail. "It's just like the one on that yellow bench by the gift shop."

"You might be on to something," said Henry. "That's good detective work, Violet."

"Now we're getting somewhere!" put in Benny.

They quickly finished their lunch, then hurried over to the gift shop to take a closer look at the bench.

"No doubt about it," said Jessie, looking from the photograph to the bench and back again. "That's the same one, all right."

They weren't really sure what they were looking for, but they set to work checking out every inch of the old bench. They found the names of tourists carved into the wood, and wads of gum stuck under the seat. But they found nothing that would help them find Patch's treasure.

Finally, Violet let out a sigh. "Looks like we struck out."

As they headed back to their cabin, Jessie

said, "Never mind, Violet. It was a good try."

"If we're on the wrong track with the bench," Henry said thoughtfully, "that can mean only one thing."

"What's that, Henry?" asked Benny as he fell into step beside his brother.

"The clue must have something to do with the cats," Henry reasoned.

"That makes sense," Jessie said after a moment's thought. "After all, there's nothing else in the—"

Suddenly a familiar voice interrupted their conversation. When they looked over, they saw Max standing on his porch with his back to them. He was talking on a cell phone. The children couldn't help overhearing bits and pieces of the conversation.

"No, no! It's important to keep this hush-hush. I don't want Abby to find out what I'm up to...I'm not sure. Maybe gold."

The children looked at each other. They didn't like the sound of this.

When Max turned and saw the Aldens, he looked startled as if he'd been caught doing something he shouldn't. "Oh, hi there!" he said, quickly pocketing his cell phone. "I was just, um…" His voice trailed away. "Guess I'd better get back inside. Got something on the stove." He was gone in a flash.

"What was that all about?" Jessie said, with a puzzled frown.

"I'm not sure," said Henry. "But it sounds like Max is up to something."

"He was talking about gold," added Benny. "Do you think he's after Patch O'Brien's treasure, too?"

"We can't be sure what Max was talking about," Violet was quick to point out.

"That's true," said Henry. "I guess we shouldn't jump to any conclusions."

"One thing's for sure," said Benny. "Things are getting more and more mysterious!"

For the rest of the day, the Aldens puzzled over the photograph. But by the time they went to bed, they were still no closer to solving the mystery.

* * * *

Around midnight, Violet awakened from a dream about Ogopogo. When she couldn't get back to sleep, she slid out of bed. She made her way over to the window and peered out at the moonlit lake. Suddenly, she gasped.

"Jessie!" she cried. "Come quick."

"What is it?" Jessie asked in a sleepy voice.

"Hurry!" Violet cried. "You've got to see this!"

Curious, Jessie threw back her covers and jumped out of bed. "See what?" she asked, coming up behind her sister.

"Look over there," Violet said in a hushed voice. "By the dock."

"I can't see any—oh!"

Violet looked over at her sister. "You can see it, too, can't you?"

Jessie nodded her head slowly, too astonished to speak.

CHAPTER 6

# *Who Goes There?*

"That's what I saw last night," Benny told them, his eyes wide with excitement. "It's Ogopogo, isn't it?"

Violet and Jessie had woken up Benny and Henry. Now they were all peering out of the bedroom window at the strange creature swimming by the dock.

"I'm not sure what it is," said Jessie.

Henry frowned. "It's kind of weird that a monster would be in the same spot two nights in a row."

"Do you think it's more than a coincidence?" asked Violet.

Henry nodded. "A lot more!"

"It does seem suspicious," said Jessie.

Henry headed for the door. "It's time to find out what's really out there on Okanagan Lake."

"*Ogopogo* Lake!" insisted Benny.

"We'll go with you, Henry," said Violet. Jessie and Benny were quick to agree.

Henry slipped quietly out of the room. So did everyone else. Henry grabbed a flashlight from the kitchen, then led the way outside. Everything was quiet and still. The only sound was the chirping of the crickets.

After tiptoeing quietly down the creaky porch steps, they hurried past the line of cabins. With the flashlight beam sweeping across the path, they headed single file down through the trees to the beach. The Aldens peered out at the dark lake. There wasn't a ripple. The strange creature had vanished.

Henry was about to say something when Benny grabbed his arm. The youngest Alden had seen something the others hadn't.

"There's somebody over there," he whispered, pointing.

Sure enough, a shadowy figure was standing near the boat.

As Henry beamed his flashlight towards the dock, Benny called out, "Who's there?"

Suddenly the figure was racing full-speed along the dock towards the water's edge. The Aldens gave chase, but it was too late. Whoever it was quickly disappeared into the trees.

They headed back to the cabin. "I don't understand it. Somebody's going to a lot of trouble to make us think there's a monster out there," said Henry.

The children had gathered in the room that Jessie and Violet were sharing. "Are you cold, Benny?" Jessie asked.

Benny, who was sitting beside Jessie on the quilted bed, was shivering. "You don't think there's *really* a monster out there? Do you?"

"No, that wasn't a monster, Benny." Henry sounded very sure.

"But how come it looked just like Ogopogo?" Benny asked as Jessie pulled a pine needle from his hair.

"I don't know how it's being done," Henry admitted. "But I'm certain it's a hoax."

Jessie agreed. "Somebody's trying to fool us."

"What I can't figure out," said Violet, perched on a trunk at the foot of the bed, "is why someone would want us to believe it was Ogopogo out there."

"I'm not sure, but I have a feeling Adam set it up," said Jessie. "This hoax, I mean."

Violet looked over at her sister. "Why would he do something like that?"

"I think I know what Jessie's getting at," said Henry. "A report of an Ogopogo sighting always brings the tourists into town, remember?"

Violet nodded her head in understanding. "You think he's hoping Abby won't sell the resort if business picks up?"

"Could be," said Jessie. "Max and Adam get a free cabin for the summer in exchange for giving boat tours. A new owner might not be willing to go along with that."

"His whole attitude changed," Jessie went on, "right after Abby said they needed a good Ogopogo sighting. Did you notice?"

Benny nodded. "He said he wasn't feeling well and hurried away."

"Exactly," said Jessie. "And then on the boat ride, he was suddenly talking as if a monster really existed."

"You know, Adam isn't the only suspect," said Violet. "I think we should add Rilla Washburn to our list."

Benny looked confused. "But...Rilla *wants* Abby to sell. Doesn't she?"

"Yes," said Violet. "But that won't happen if we find the treasure."

"You think Rilla's trying to distract us?" asked Henry. "Is that what you mean, Violet?"

"It's possible," said Violet. "Maybe she figures we'll start hunting for Ogopogo and forget all about the treasure."

"But Rilla doesn't believe that Patch left a

treasure," Benny pointed out, looking even more confused.

"Maybe that's just what she wants *us* to believe," Henry said. He was leaning against the pine dresser, his arms folded. "Maybe she's afraid the treasure might be worth enough to save the resort."

Benny spoke up. "I know somebody we should put at the top of our list of suspects."

"You're thinking of Max, right?" guessed Jessie.

"I bet he's the one trying to distract us," Benny said, nodding. "He wants to beat us to the treasure."

Jessie had to admit Benny had a point. "Max did say something about gold when he was talking on the phone."

Violet frowned. "We want to be sure he was talking about the treasure." She liked Max and couldn't imagine him trying to take Abby's treasure from her.

"Oh, Max is up to something, all right," insisted Henry. "I'm just not sure it has anything to do with the treasure."

"But it's true, Henry," said Benny, who wasn't about to let go of his idea. "Max wants the treasure for himself."

"If we prove it, it's true, Benny," Jessie corrected. "Until then, it's just a theory."

Violet let out a sigh. "It's hard to know who to trust."

"I think we should watch them closely for a while," suggested Henry. "Max, Adam, and Rilla."

"But let's keep a lid on this for now," Jessie said with a yawn. "We'll try to figure out a few things on our own."

With that, they put the mystery out of their minds as they went back to bed and drifted off to sleep.

* * * *

The four Alden children were up bright and early the next morning. Remembering their promise to Abby to paint the signs, they headed off to town right after breakfast.

"What do you think of purple for the lettering on the signs?" Violet asked as they browsed around the paint store.

"Sounds good," said Jessie, who was looking at a color chart. "How about this one? It's called Lavender Mist."

"Plum Delight is really nice, too," put in Violet. Purple was her favorite color, and she almost always wore something purple or violet. "There are so many colors, it's hard to choose."

It took awhile, but the four Aldens finally decided on Lavender Mist, Goldenrod Yellow, and Dragonfly Blue.

"Is it lunchtime yet?" Benny asked as they stood at the check-out.

Henry looked at his watch. "Close enough," he said. "I noticed a diner on our way over here."

No sooner had they stepped outside than Rilla Washburn came round the corner. She was wearing a green dress and matching earrings. She seemed to be in a big hurry, but when she caught sight of the Aldens, she slowed down.

"Well, if it isn't the gold hunters," she said, "or have you thrown in the towel already?"

Henry shook his head. "We don't give up that easily."

Rilla's smile disappeared. "You're wasting your time," she said. "Look, I know what I'm talking about. There's no treasure. End of story."

"But we already figured out something," Benny piped up. "Jessie, show Rilla the photograph of Patch's cats in your backpack. There's a clue hidden in the photograph of—" Just then, he noticed Jessie's warning frown. He'd forgotten they weren't supposed to talk about the mystery.

Rilla caught the look. "Oh, come now," she said. "You can tell me about it. Your secret's safe with me."

"We have to go," said Jessie, pointing to her watch. "Sorry."

"You're getting Abby's hopes up for nothing with this little game of yours!" Rilla snapped at them.

This was too much for Jessie. "We're trying to help," she said, looking Rilla straight in the eye.

"Well, you're not!" Rilla shot back, getting more annoyed by the minute. "You're not helping one bit!" With that, she hurried off.

# CHAPTER 7

## *Meow!*

"Can you believe that?" Jessie said as they headed down the street. "Rilla acts like we're doing something wrong."

"She doesn't want us hunting for the treasure," Henry added as they stepped inside the diner. "That's for sure."

Violet nodded. "She's afraid Abby won't sell the resort if we find something valuable."

Jessie nodded. "And that means Rilla would be runner-up again for the top sales award."

As they settled into a booth, Benny said, "She was wondering if we gave up already. We never give up."

"Rilla sure doesn't know us very well." Henry smiled over at his little brother.

Jessie passed out the menus. "Did you notice that Rilla called us *gold* hunters?"

"Hey, Max was talking about gold when he was on the phone!" Benny realized.

"Could just be a coincidence," said Henry.

But Jessie wasn't so sure. Her mind was racing. "Unless—"

"Unless what, Jessie?" Henry questioned.

"Unless Max and Rilla are working together."

The others looked at Jessie in surprise. "You think it was Rilla on the other end of the line?" Violet asked.

"It's possible." Jessie nodded. "If Max finds the treasure first, he'll make some quick cash, and—"

"And Abby would have no choice but to sell the resort!" Henry finished his sister's sentence for her. "It would work out very well for both Rilla *and* Max," he added.

Benny folded his arms, "That means there's only one thing to do," he said in a very serious voice. "Find the treasure first!"

"You're right, Benny." Jessie pulled the photograph of Patch O'Brien's cats from her backpack. "But we won't find it until we figure out what this photograph is trying to tell us."

Just then, a young woman with a cheery smile came over to take their orders. "What'll it be, kids?"

Henry chose a ham sandwich and lemonade. Violet and Jessie both ordered grilled cheese sandwiches, coleslaw, and milk. Benny decided on chicken nuggets, fries, and a root-beer float.

Jessie couldn't help noticing that the waitress kept looking over at the photograph as she took their orders. Why was she so interested in a picture of seven cats curled up on a bench?

"That should do for starters," said Benny, closing the menu.

The other Aldens looked at each other and smiled. They could always count on their little brother to have a big appetite.

The waitress gave Benny a wink. "Our chocolate cream pie is a big favorite around here."

"Do we have enough money for dessert, Henry?" asked Benny.

"Are you sure you'll have enough room?" Henry smiled as he waited for his younger brother's answer, even though he knew what it would be.

"I always have room for dessert," said Benny, who had a sweet tooth.

At this, the waitress couldn't help laughing. She added chocolate cream pie to their order, then walked away.

As they waited for their food to arrive, the Aldens turned their attention to the photograph of Patch O'Brien's cats.

"Just what are those cats trying to tell us?" Henry wondered. He was still convinced they were some kind of clue.

Benny had an opinion. "I think I know

what they're saying. They're saying—meow!"

They all burst out laughing at Benny's joke. "I have a feeling there's more to it than that, Sherlock," Henry said.

The four Aldens were quiet for a while as they peered long and hard at the photograph. There were seven cats altogether, and each one was different. One was black, one was charcoal-gray. One was small and honey-colored, one was big and brown. One had white-tipped ears, one had a striped tail. And there was one that was a big ball of orange fur.

"I don't get it," Violet said at last. "Do you?" She looked around at the others.

Benny shook his head. "I don't see anything that looks like a clue."

"I've drawn a blank, too," Henry admitted. "This is going to be a tough one to figure out."

Jessie agreed. "All we really know is that Patch loved cats."

"He sure did."

The children turned to see the waitress standing over them, looking at the photograph.

"I couldn't help noticing," she said as she placed their food on the table. "Aren't those Patch O'Brien's cats?"

"Yes," Jessie said in surprise. "Did you know Patch O'Brien?"

"Everyone around here knew Patch," said the waitress. "Real outdoorsy type. He stopped by the diner every now and again." She laughed a little. "Always ordered a slab of apple pie and a cup of coffee. My name's Tory, by the way. Short for Victoria."

Jessie returned Tory's friendly smile. "I'm Jessie, and this is Violet, Henry, and Benny." She pointed to her sister and brothers in turn.

After saying hello, Tory went on, "When Patch died, I took in Chad and Coco." She pointed to the photograph. "Chad's the one with the white tips on his ears. And see the big brown one? That's Coco."

"Cute names for cats," said Jessie.

Tory nodded. "My sister adopted Custard and Charlie. Custard's the black one, and Charlie's the one with the striped tail. Now, the gray cat—that's Crumpet. The owner of the gas station took her in."

"Chad, Coco, Custard, Charlie, and Crumpet." Benny was counting on his fingers. "That makes five," he pointed out. "What about the other two?" The others were wondering the same thing.

Tory thought for a moment. "I believe the orange cat and that little honey-colored one both went to a family on the edge of town."

Benny had another question. "What were their names?" he asked. "The cats, I mean. Not the family."

"Hmm, now just what were their names?" Tory was tapping a pen thoughtfully against her chin when a young couple came into the diner. As she hurried off, she called back to the Aldens, "Don't worry, it'll come to me. It's on the tip of my tongue!"

Benny was just dipping his last french fry into ketchup when Tory came back. "Clem and Chelsey," she said, looking pleased with herself. "Clem was the orange cat, and Chelsey was the honey-colored one."

Violet giggled. She couldn't help it. "They all have names beginning with the letter *C.*"

"We always thought it was strange." Tory chuckled. "But the names are fun to say all together—Clem, Chelsey, Custard, Charlie, Coco, Chad, and Crumpet."

"I wonder why Patch did that," said Jessie. "Gave all his cats names beginning with the letter *C,* I mean."

"Well, he always did like the sea," Tory said, her eyes twinkling.

Everyone laughed—except Benny.

"I don't get it," he said, as the waitress walked away.

"Tory was making a joke," Henry explained to his little brother. "Patch liked the kind of sea you go sailing on. Maybe that's why he liked the letter *C.*"

"Oh," said Benny, who still wasn't sure what was so funny.

"Seven cats—all with names beginning

with the letter *C*," said Henry. He was deep in thought as he pushed the salt shaker around on the table.

Violet looked at him. "Do you think it means something, Henry?"

"I have the weirdest feeling that we're close to figuring something out." Henry paused for a moment to sort out his thoughts. "I just can't quite put my finger on what it is."

CHAPTER 8

# A Purr-fect Solution

Back at the resort, the Alden children found their grandfather sitting on the cabin porch with Abby.

"How did you make out in town?" Grandfather asked.

"We got everything we'll need for the signs," said Henry, handing Abby the change. "Sandpaper, brushes, and paint."

Violet nodded. "Wait till you see the great colors we chose!"

"Well, those signs can use a bit of pizazz.

But are you sure you want to spend your time working?" asked Abby.

Grandfather laughed. "You don't know these children, Abby. There's nothing they like better than hard work."

"Well, then it's okay. Oh, by the way," said Abby, "any luck with the riddle?"

Jessie didn't want to lie, but she didn't want to get Abby's hopes up, either. "We're still working on it," she said.

"I wouldn't spend too much time on it if I were you," Abby advised. "I'm sure Rilla's right. There probably isn't any treasure at all."

But the Aldens weren't convinced Rilla was right. They had a strong hunch there *was* a treasure. And it was a treasure just waiting to be found.

After a swim in the lake and a game of horseshoes with Adam, they got to work on the signs. Sitting in the shade of an elm, they sanded the rough spots where the paint was chipped and peeling. Henry worked on the sign for THE OGOPOGO GIFT SHOP.

Jessie tackled CABINS FOR RENT. And Violet and Benny worked on THE OGO-POGO RESORT.

Jessie had just brought out a thermos of lemonade when she noticed something that made her frown. "That's odd," she said. "Didn't Patch carve an Ogopogo for every porch?"

"That's right." Henry said. "At least, that's what Abby said."

Violet asked, "What's odd about that?"

Jessie gestured toward the line of cabins. "Take a look at the porch on the far right."

They all followed Jessie's gaze. "Oh," said Violet. "I see what you mean, Jessie. No carving."

"Maybe Abby sold it," guessed Violet.

"Everything Patch made sold like hot-cakes. Remember?" said Henry.

"Still, it is kind of weird," insisted Jessie. "I'm sure that carving was on the porch when we arrived."

"You know what I think?" added Benny. "I think the number seven is a clue."

"What makes you say that, Benny?" Henry questioned.

"For one thing, Patch had seven cats," Benny explained. "And for another thing, cats have seven lives."

"Nine," Jessie corrected.

"What?"

"Cats have *nine* lives, Benny," Jessie told him. "At least, that's how the saying goes."

"Nine?" Benny scratched his head. "Are you sure?"

Nodding, Jessie smiled at her little brother.

"You know what, Benny?" said Henry. "I think you're on to something with the number seven. After all, there are seven cats with seven names that begin with the letter *C*."

Benny nodded. "Clem, Chelsey, Custard, Charlie, Coco, Chad, and Crumpet."

"Very good, Benny!" praised Jessie.

The youngest Alden beamed. "A detective always remembers stuff like that."

"You think it's some kind of clue, Henry?" Violet wondered.

"Got to be," said Henry. "I just can't shake the feeling those seven *C's* must mean something." Just then, he clapped a hand over his mouth, surprised by his own words.

"What are you thinking, Henry?" asked Jessie.

"I'm thinking we should check out Patch O'Brien's boat," answered Henry.

"Why do you say that, Henry?" Violet asked.

"Think about it." Henry looked around at his brother and sisters. "What's the name of Abby's boat?"

"The *Seven Seas*," Jessie said, puzzled. Then her face brightened as she suddenly caught on. "The seven cats all have names that start with a *C*—the seven *C's!*"

"The cats are pointing the way to the boat!" Benny let out a cheer. Solving clues was always fun.

"You think there's something hidden on the *Seven Seas*?" Voilet asked.

"Let's go find out." Henry scrambled to

his feet. "Max said we were welcome on the *Seven Seas* anytime. And there's no time like right now," he added.

Henry, Jessie, Violet, and Benny put on life jackets and hurried down to the lake. They wasted no time climbing aboard the *Seven Seas*. As they began to look around, Jessie spoke up.

"Remember," she said, "anything that looks unusual can be a clue."

The others gave Jessie the thumbs-up. They were determined to check out every inch of the boat. But it wasn't long before Benny found something.

"Come look!" he called out.

Henry, Jessie, and Benny hurried over.

Benny had removed the life jackets stowed in the compartment under the bench seat. He was staring down into the empty bin.

"What is it?" asked Henry.

"I think I just found a clue!" Benny sounded excited.

The others crowded around. Sure enough,

a message had been carved into the wood at the bottom of the storage bin.

"Benny, you're an awesome detective!" Jessie said proudly.

"I guess I am." Benny grinned from ear to ear. "But...what does it say?"

Jessie read the strange message aloud.

> *Backwards or forwards,*
> *from left or from right,*
> *it's always the same,*
> *by day or by night.*

"Patch sure made hard riddles," said Benny.

Jessie began to copy the riddle in her notebook. "I just hope we can figure this one out."

"What's the same backwards or forwards?" Benny said, after a moment's thought.

Nobody had any ideas. It seemed like the more they looked for answers, the more questions they had.

# CHAPTER 9

# Getting Warmer

"Abby told me about a family park nearby," Grandfather said over breakfast the next morning. "They have bumper boats and go-karts and miniature golfing. Anybody interested in checking it out?"

"That'd be great!" cried Benny, his eyes shining.

Henry agreed. "That's a super idea, Grandfather," he said, every bit as excited as his little brother. "Besides, we could use a break from detective work." The four Alden children had puzzled and puzzled over the latest riddle. But by the time they'd gone to bed, they still hadn't come up with any answers.

"I promised Abby I'd join her for a cup of coffee before we leave," said Grandfather, taking the blueberry muffins that Violet passed to him. "But it won't take long."

After breakfast, the four Alden children cleared the table and washed the dishes while Grandfather had coffee with Abby.

"Let's take your notebook with us, Jessie," suggested Violet, who was giving the counters a once-over. "We can try to figure out the riddle on the drive."

"I was thinking the same thing," Henry agreed. "We really don't have time to take a break from this mystery."

"I put the notebook in my backpack," said Jessie, glancing around the room. "Now...where did I leave the backpack?"

Violet looked around, too. "Maybe it's outside. The last time I remember seeing it was when we were painting the signs."

Benny was already halfway to the door. "I bet we left it by that big tree."

The Aldens wasted no time checking it out. Sure enough, Jessie's denim backpack was leaning up against the trunk of the old elm tree.

"It's right where we left—oh, no!" Benny exclaimed.

"What in the world...?" Violet cried out at the same time.

The four Aldens stared in astonishment. The words MIND YOUR OWN BUSI-NESS—OR ELSE! had been painted in purple across one of the signboards.

Henry gave a low whistle. "Somebody sure doesn't want us looking for that treasure."

Benny's eyes were huge. "Who do you think...?"

"Could be anybody," Jessie broke in as she fished through the denim backpack for her notebook.

Henry used a stick to pry open the lid on the can of Goldenrod Yellow. "It'll take more than a message in purple to get us to back off," he said. Then he grabbed a paint brush and slapped a thick coat of Goldenrod Yellow over the words.

"It's gone!" Jessie suddenly cried out.

Henry looked up. "What's gone?"

"Are you talking about your notebook, Jessie?" Violet wanted to know.

Jessie shook her head. "My notebook is here, but...the photograph is gone!"

"Are you positive you left it in your backpack?" Henry wanted to make sure.

"Yes," said Jessie. "It was right in this zippered pocket with the notebook."

"I don't understand." Violet frowned. "It couldn't just disappear."

"It could if somebody stole it," Benny said. "And I bet it was the same person who left that message."

"Oh, Benny!" Violet exclaimed. "Why would anyone steal an old photograph of cats?"

"Unless," Jessie remarked, "he—or she— knew the photo held a clue to the treasure."

"Uh-oh," said Benny.

Henry looked over at his little brother. "What is it, Benny?"

"Rilla Washburn knew about the clue," Benny said in a quiet voice. "I gave away top-secret information when we saw her in town. Remember?"

"That's okay, Benny," Jessie assured him. "At least the thief didn't take my notebook."

The children forgot all about the mystery for a while when they got to the amusement park. They rode the bumper boats and the go-karts and did some wall climbing. Even Grandfather joined them for a game of miniature golf. Everyone had a wonderful time—at least until they were heading back to the resort. When they stopped at a café for lunch, Grandfather told them the news.

"It seems Abby's made up her mind," he said after the waitress had brought their food. They'd all ordered the special—cold turkey sandwiches, homemade potato chips, and root beer. "She's decided to sell the Ogopogo Resort."

"What...?" Benny almost choked on a potato chip.

"Oh, no!" Violet cried at the same time.

"I'm afraid it's true," said Grandfather. As he took a sip of root beer, the ice cubes clinked in the glass. "She told me this morning."

The four Aldens looked at each other in dismay. They'd been so sure they'd find the treasure in time!

Grandfather swallowed a bite of his sandwich. "She's planning to put in a call to her real estate agent today."

"*Today?*" Henry winced.

"Abby's made up her mind," said Grandfather. "I told her I'd look over the sales contract with her. It's important to check out the small print."

Benny frowned. "But we were getting warmer."

Grandfather smiled at his youngest grandson. "I know you were hoping to save the day, Benny," he said. "But things don't always work out the way we plan."

Violet let out a sigh. "I just wish things weren't working out the way Rilla planned."

"Abby hasn't sold the resort yet, Violet," Jessie reminded her, before crunching into a potato chip.

"That's true," said Henry. "And we haven't given up yet, have we?"

"No!" the other Aldens almost shouted.

True to their word, the moment they got back to the resort, the four children turned their attention once again to the latest riddle.

To refresh their memories, Jessie pulled out her notebook and began to recite, *Backwards or forwards, / from left or from right, / it's always the same, / by day or by night.*

Nobody said anything. They were deep in thought as they continued to paint signs.

"I still don't get it," Benny said, dipping his brush into the can of Lavender Mist. "What's the same backwards or forwards?"

Violet couldn't help laughing when she looked over at her little brother. "Oh, Benny!" she said. "You look like you've been face-painting."

The youngest Alden had a smear of Goldenrod Yellow on his chin, a drop of Dragonfly Blue on the tip of his nose, and a splattering of Lavender Mist on his forehead.

"Paint likes my face," said Benny, making them all laugh.

"I think paint likes your clothes, too," Henry joked, making them laugh even harder.

Just then, they heard the crunch of tires on gravel. They looked over to see Max getting out of his car. Smiling, he came across the grass, carrying a package under his arm.

"Great job!" He looked down at the signs approvingly. "They'll be real easy to spot now."

Benny gave him a half-hearted smile. "It won't really matter."

"Yeah, I heard the news." Max stopped smiling. "I kept hoping Abby wouldn't sell, but..." His words trailed away.

"We were all hoping Abby wouldn't sell," put in Jessie.

"Listen," said Max. He lowered his voice as if about to share a secret. "I could use your opinion on something." Taking the package from under his arm, he tore away the wrapping. "What do you think?" he asked, holding up a painting in a wood frame.

"That's a picture of this place," Benny realized. "And you can even see Ogopogo Lake in the background."

Max looked puzzled. "Ogopogo Lake?"

"That's what Benny calls Okanagan Lake," Jessie explained.

"It's a beautiful painting," said Violet, taking a closer look. The watercolor showed a row of cabins nestled amongst the trees, with a lake in the background. "Oh—look at the bottom corner!"

"That's Patch O'Brien's signature." Max was beaming.

Henry gave Max a questioning look. "Abby's friend painted that?"

Max nodded. "I found it in our cabin—shoved in the back of a closet," he said. "I got it framed to surprise Abby."

"She'll love it," Jessie said, and the others nodded.

"You think the frame's okay, then?" Max wanted to know.

Violet said, "That dark wood is perfect for the painting."

"I thought so, too," said Max, looking relieved. "At first, I thought a gold frame would be best. But then, on a hunch, I went with the dark wood."

The Aldens exchanged glances. A *gold* frame? That must have been the phone conversation they'd overheard.

"I'll give it to Abby tonight," Max went on, "after Rilla Washburn leaves. I'm hoping this little surprise will cheer her up a bit."

Violet nodded in sudden understanding. That's what Max had meant about keeping things hush-hush. He had wanted the painting to be a surprise.

"Our lips are sealed," Henry promised.

"Looks like that's one suspect we can cross off our list," Jessie said when Max was out of earshot.

Nodding, Violet smiled a little. She knew Max could never be Rilla's partner in crime.

"I'm almost finished here," Henry said, dabbing his brush into Dragonfly Blue paint.

"Me, too," said Jessie.

"Violet and I just have the letters for OGO-POGO left," Benny put in. "We already did RESORT."

"How about this, Benny?" said Violet. "I'll paint the letters O—G—O at the beginning, and you paint the letters O—G—O at the end."

"Sure," Benny agreed. "And we can both do the letter P in the middle."

Violet couldn't help laughing. "Did you notice? OGOPOGO is spelled the same both ways."

Benny took another look. "Hey, you're right, Violet!" he said in surprise. "That's kind of funny, isn't it?"

"It's called a palindrome," said Jessie.

"A palin-what?" Benny asked.

"Palindrome," Jessie repeated. "That's a word that's spelled the same backwards or—"

"Forwards!" finished Henry, snapping his fingers. He sounded excited.

Violet and Benny looked over at their older brother and sister, puzzled.

"Remember the riddle?" Jessie explained, slapping Henry a high-five. *"Backwards or forwards, / from left or from right, / it's always the same, / by day or by night."*

"Wait a minute," cried Benny. *"Ogopogo* is the answer to the riddle? Is that what you mean, Jessie?"

Jessie nodded. "That's exactly what I mean, Benny."

"Yeah!" shouted the youngest Alden. So did the others.

"But what does Ogopogo have to do with the treasure?" Violet wondered.

Benny's face lit up. "I bet the treasure's hidden in one of Ogopogo's underwater caves!"

"Could be," said Henry. "But I have a feeling it's closer than that."

"Do you think it's on the property some-where, Henry?" Violet wanted to know.

Henry didn't seem to hear the question. He was busy fishing around in the can of purple paint. "That's weird," he said. "There's something floating in here."

Curious, the other Aldens moved closer. Henry removed a small object from the can. It was dripping with paint.

"What is that?" Benny wanted to know.

"I'm not sure." Henry reached for a rag to wipe away the paint. "Looks like jewelry."

"What's jewelry doing in a can of purple paint?" Benny asked as Henry held up a long, dangly earring.

"Wait a minute," said Violet, leaning in closer. "Are those green stones?"

Henry grabbed the rag and gave the earring another once-over. "Yeah, the stones are definitely green."

Jessie turned to her younger sister. "What are you thinking, Violet?"

"It looks familiar," Violet said. "I've seen that earring somewhere before."

Just then, another car pulled into the driveway. They watched as Rilla

Washburn climbed out and made a beeline for the gift shop.

"Of course!" Violet cried. "Rilla was wearing the same earrings. When we ran into her in town, I mean."

"Are you sure about that, Violet?" Henry asked.

Violet nodded her head up and down. "I remember how well the stones matched her dress."

"But…how did Rilla's earring get into the paint?" Benny wanted to know.

Henry had an answer. "It probably fell in when she was leaving that message."

"Right before she stole the picture of Patch's cats out of Jessie's backpack," added Violet.

"You think Rilla is the person who left the message telling us to mind our own business—or else, *and* stole the picture?" asked Jessie.

"It had to be her," Henry insisted. "How else can you explain her earring getting into the paint?"

"Shouldn't we tell Abby?" Benny wondered.

"The problem is," Jessie told her little brother. "we can't *prove* the earring belongs to Rilla."

"And she'd never admit it was hers," added Violet. "Otherwise, she'd have to explain how it got into the paint."

"Maybe she doesn't even know that's what happened," Henry said. "Let's tell her we found her earring and see what happens."

# CHAPTER 10

# Case Closed

The children could hear voices in the living room. "Something's come up," Henry said as they went in.

"What is it, Henry?" asked Grandfather. He was sitting on the couch, with Rilla Washburn perched in a chair nearby. "Is anything wrong?"

Henry shook his head. "No, but—"

"Well, if nothing's wrong," Rilla cut in sharply, "I suggest you come back later. We're trying to have a business meeting here."

"We're sorry to interrupt," said Jessie, who was always polite. "We'll be out of your way in a minute."

Henry held the earring out to Rilla in the palm of his hand. "We thought this might be yours."

"Oh!" Rilla's face perked up. "I've been looking everywhere for that." She snatched the earring from Henry's hand. "Where did you find it?"

"In a can of paint," Henry answered, watching her closely.

"What...?" A funny look came over Rilla's face. "Why, I can't imagine how—"

Henry cut in, "Maybe it fell in when you were leaving that message for us."

"On one of Abby's signboards," added Benny, his hands on his hips.

"A message on a signboard?" Rilla lifted her hands as if she was confused. "I'm afraid I don't know what you're talking about."

"It was a message telling us to mind our own business," Jessie reminded her, "or else!"

"Oh, my goodness!" A look of shock crossed Abby's face. "What is this about?"

"You think I'd do such a thing, Abby?" Rilla looked hurt. "I have no idea what these kids are up to," she added, "but you can be sure they didn't find this earring in a can of purple paint!"

"Nobody said it was *purple* paint," Violet said quietly. "How did you know that?"

"Uh, well…I, er…" Rilla struggled to find something to say.

"Rilla!" Abby cried. "Is this true? Did you leave a threatening message for these children?"

Rilla opened her mouth, then closed it again. Finally, she slumped back against the cushions. "Yes, I did leave that message, and I feel terrible about it." She lowered her head and sniffed, pretending to cry.

Abby was so startled, she needed a few moments to collect her thoughts. "But…why?"

"That's just what I was wondering," Grandfather said sternly.

Rilla looked up and gave a little smile.

"It's really not such a big deal, is it?"

"You wanted us to stop looking for the treasure, didn't you?" guessed Violet.

Rilla didn't deny it. "Treasure-hunting does sound harmless," she said. "But I knew it would cause problems later on."

"Problems?" Abby looked even more confused. "What kind of problems?"

Jessie spoke up. "If we found the treasure, there'd be no reason for you to sell the resort, Abby."

"And if you didn't sell the resort to Rilla, then she would miss out on the top sales award *again*," added Henry.

"That's why Rilla was trying to scare us by leaving us that message, and why she stole the picture Patch left Abby with the riddle leading to the treasure," added Violet.

"What?" Rilla exclaimed. "I did nothing of the sort!" Rilla began to defend herself and then quickly gave up as she saw that everyone in the room knew what she had done.

"Fine," she said. "When Benny mentioned Jessie had a photo in her backpack with a clue to the treasure written on it, I decided to take it." Rilla reached into her purse, pulled out the old snapshot, and handed it to Abby. "I couldn't let anything get in the way of this sale! I've missed out on the top sales award too many times, and if I sold this resort, nothing could stop me from winning," Rilla explained.

Abby looked hurt. "You know how much this resort means to me, Rilla. I would have hoped our friendship was more important to you than the top sales award."

Rilla sat quietly.

"And that's not all," Benny chimed in. "Rilla even made a fake monster to scare us away!"

"No, I didn't do any such thing!" Rilla's dark eyes suddenly flashed. "I don't know anything about a fake monster."

The Aldens looked at each other. They had a feeling Rilla was telling the truth.

"I did leave that message and I stole the

picture, but that's all," she went on. "I'm so sorry, Abby. I never meant for this to go so far."

"Sorry isn't enough," said Abby. "I draw the line at leaving threatening messages for children."

"You're right, Abby. I did get carried away," said Rilla. "But the resort still needs to be sold. My client made you a good offer."

Abby got to her feet. "I'll have to pass."

Rilla waved away Abby's words. "Now, none of that. We can't let friendship get in the way of business, can we?" she said. "Or business get in the way of friendship, for that matter."

Abby had heard enough. "You and I have different ideas about friendship, Rilla. I'm afraid I must ask you to leave."

"You can't mean it!"

"Yes, I do, Rilla." Abby folded her arms, a no-nonsense look on her face.

"Fine!" Rilla headed for the door. As she left, she called back, "You won't be seeing me around here again!"

"I'm counting on it," replied Abby.

As the door slammed shut, Grandfather said, "I guess that's that."

"Actually, it's a load off my mind, James." Abby sat down again. "I really wasn't ready to sell the resort. Not just yet, anyway."

"Is the coast clear?" asked Max, sticking his head into the room.

Nodding, Abby gestured for him to come in. "Rilla's gone."

Max stepped into the room, the painting tucked under his arm. Adam was close behind.

"It didn't take you long to close the deal, Abby," Max remarked, pulling up a chair.

"I decided not to sell the resort, Max."

Max and Adam stared at Abby in surprise. "You mean, you still own the Ogopogo Resort?" Adam wanted to know.

"For the moment, at least." Abby quickly explained what had happened. She finished by saying, "When I do sell the resort, it won't be with Rilla Washburn's agency. You can be sure of that."

"Well, Adam and I brought you a present," said Max. "We figured it would help cheer you up."

"For me?" Abby wasted no time tearing the wrapping away from the package Max handed her. When she caught sight of the painting, she caught her breath. "Oh, my!"

"Well, look at that!" said Grandfather, admiringly. "It's the Ogopogo Resort."

"And look!" Abby cried out with delight. "There's Patch O'Brien's signature in the corner!"

"We found it in the cabin," Adam told her. "So we got it framed."

"Thank you so much!" Abby gave them each a warm hug. "Now I'll have two wonderful treasures."

"Two?" Benny looked puzzled.

"I'm talking about the painting and my wonderful Ogopogo." Abby looked at the carving of Ogopogo beside the fireplace resting on a special wooden stand.

"Omigosh!" exclaimed Jessie.

The others turned to look at her. "What's the matter, Jessie?"

"I know where the treasure is!" she told them in an awestruck voice.

"Where?" Henry wanted to know.

Everyone followed her gaze to the carving of Ogopogo on the wooden stand.

"I don't get it," said Violet. "You think the carving is the treasure? Is that what you mean, Jessie?"

"No, Violet." Jessie shook her head. "I think the treasure's hidden *inside* the carving."

"There's just one catch, Jessie," said Abby. "There's no way Patch could hide anything inside that Ogopogo carving. It's made from solid wood."

"Oh." Jessie's face fell. Still, she couldn't shake the feeling they were on the right track.

Henry had been thinking. "Unless..."

"Unless what, Henry?" Violet wanted to know.

It took Henry a moment to answer.

"Unless the treasure's hidden inside the stand."

"Do you mind if we check it out, Abby?" Jessie asked.

"My grandchildren are seldom wrong when it comes to solving mysteries," Grandfather was quick to add.

"Go for it!" Abby exclaimed as everyone gathered round. "Hurry, I can't stand the suspense!"

"Careful now," said Max, giving Henry a hand. Together, they managed to tip the carving onto its side.

Henry knelt down, then rapped his knuckles against the stand. "Sounds hollow."

Jessie noticed something. "Isn't that a hole on the bottom?" She crouched down beside her older brother to get a closer look.

Henry nodded. "Just big enough for my finger."

"I've got a pencil box with a lid that slides open," said Violet. "Maybe the bottom of the stand slides open, too."

"It's worth a try." Henry stuck his finger

into the hole and pushed with all his might. The base of the stand jerked a little to the side. He pushed again. This time, the base slid far enough to leave a small opening.

"That should do the trick," said Grandfather.

Henry reached into the hollow stand and patted all around.

"Can you feel anything, Henry?" Benny was bouncing from one foot to the other.

Henry shook his head. "I don't—wait!"

Everyone gasped when Henry pulled out a red velvet pouch. "I think this belongs to you, Abby." He stood up straight and held it out to her.

"Oh, my!" cried Abby.

"That's not a very *big* pouch," said Benny, who sounded a bit disappointed.

Jessie smiled over at her little brother. "You know what they say, Benny," she reminded him. "Good things come in small packages."

"Well, let's find out if that old saying is true," said Abby. She took a deep breath,

then shook the contents of the pouch onto the coffee table.

For a moment, no one said a word. They just stared in amazement. Then Violet whispered, "Diamonds!"

Abby sank back against the cushions. "Bless his heart!" she said, in a daze. "Patch really did find treasure on a sunken ship, after all!"

"Those diamonds must be worth a small fortune," said Max.

"You'll have more than enough money to fix up the resort, Abby," Adam told her.

"And pay for some advertising," added Grandfather.

Abby clasped her hands together. "Yes, it looks like I'll be keeping the old place after all."

"Your grandchildren really saved the day, James," said Abby. Her smile made the four Aldens feel warm all over.

But something was still bothering Violet. "If Rilla wasn't behind the Ogopogo hoax, then who was?"

"That was me," Adam said in a small voice.

All eyes turned to him. "What's this all about?" asked Max.

Adam blurted out the truth. "I wanted the Aldens to think they'd seen Ogopogo."

"But...how?" Violet's eyebrows furrowed.

Adam looked over at her. "You're wondering how I did it?"

Violet nodded. "It looked just like—oh!" she cried in sudden understanding. "You used one of Patch's carvings, didn't you?"

Adam didn't deny it. "I put the carving on the raft, and floated it out into the water." Then he glanced over at Abby sheepishly. "I just borrowed it from one of the cabins, Abby. I planned to put it back."

"I don't understand," said Abby. "Why would you try to fool the Aldens?"

"That's what *I'd* like to know," Max added with a frown.

Henry thought he knew the answer to that. "You thought we'd report it to the newspaper, didn't you?"

"I was hoping a sighting would bring tourists into town," Adam confessed.

Jessie nodded in understanding. No wonder Adam seemed to have changed his mind overnight. He didn't believe Ogopogo was real, but he wanted the Aldens to believe it did.

"Oh, I get it," said Max. "You figured if business picked up, then Abby wouldn't sell the resort."

Adam nodded. "I hadn't counted on the Aldens figuring out it was a hoax."

"I know your heart was in the right place, Adam," said Abby. "But it's never a good thing to fool people."

Adam looked truly sorry. "I guess I made a big mistake."

"Everybody makes mistakes." Henry told him. "We'll be here until the end of the week," he added with a friendly smile. "Maybe we can make a fresh start."

Adam smiled. "I'd like that."

Abby looked at Adam. "You made a mistake because you were trying to be a friend, and I'm so lucky to have so many friends care about me so much."

"There's no treasure better than a good friend!" said Benny. "Right?"

"Right!" everyone answered together.

GERTRUDE CHANDLER WARNER discovered when she was teaching that many readers who like an exciting story could find no books that were both easy and fun to read. She decided to try to meet this need, and her first book, *The Boxcar Children*, quickly proved she had succeeded.

Miss Warner drew on her own experiences to write the mystery. As a child she spent hours watching trains go by on the tracks opposite her family home. She often dreamed about what it would be like to set up housekeeping in a caboose or freight car—the situation the Alden children find themselves in.

While the mystery element is central to each of Miss Warner's books, she never thought of them as strictly juvenile mysteries. She liked to stress the Aldens' independence and resourcefulness and their solid New England devotion to using up and making do. The Aldens go about most of their adventures with as little adult supervision as possible—something else that delights young readers.

Miss Warner lived in Putnam, Connecticut, until her death in 1979. During her lifetime, she received hundreds of letters from girls and boys telling her how much they liked her books.